GRIZZLY!

AS TOLD TO BEN EAST

ILLUSTRATED & DESIGNED BY JACK DAHL

EDITED BY JEROLYN NENTL AND DR. HOWARD SCHROEDER

Professor in Reading and Language Arts, Dept. of Elementary Education, Mankato State University

Library of Congress Cataloging in Publication Data

East, Ben
  Grizzly! As told to Ben East.
  (Survival)
  SUMMARY: A man's realization of his desire to meet face-to-face with
a grizzly bear changes some of his previous ideas about them.
  1. Grizzly bear--Juvenile literature. (1. Grizzly bear. 2. Bears) I. Dahl,
John I. II. Nentl, Jerolyn Ann. III. Schroeder, Howard. IV. Title. V. Series.
QL737.G22E23   599'.74446   79-53748
ISBN 0-89686-045-0 lib. bdg.
ISBN 0-89686-053-1 pbk.

International Standard Book Numbers: **Library of Congress**
   0-89686-045-0 Library Bound   **Catalog Number:**
   0-89686-053-1 Paperback   79-53748

ABOUT THE AUTHOR...

Ben East has been an *Outdoor Life* staff editor since 1946. Born in southeastern Michigan in 1898, and a lifelong resident of that state, he sold his first story to *Outers Recreation* (later absorbed by *Outdoor Life*) in 1921. In 1926 he began a career as a professional writer, becoming outdoor editor of Booth Newspapers, a chain of dailies in eight major Michigan cities outside Detroit.

He left the newspaper job on January 1, 1946, to become Midwest field editor of Outdoor Life. In 1966 he was advanced to senior field editor, a post from which he retired at the end of 1970. Since then he has continued to write for the magazine as a contributing field editor.

Growing up as a farm boy, he began fishing and hunting as soon as he could handle a cane pole and a .22 rifle. He has devoted sixty years to outdoor sports, travel, adventure, wildlife photography, writing and lecturing. Ben has covered much of the back country of North America, from the eastern seaboard to the Aleutian Islands of Alaska, and from the Canadian arctic to the southern United States. He has written more than one thousand magazine articles and eight books. Today his by-line is one of the best known of any outdoor writer in the country. His outstanding achievement in wildlife photography was the making of the first color film ever taken of the Alaskan sea otter, in the summer of 1941.

In recent years much of his writing has dealt with major conservation problems confronting the nation. He has produced hard-hitting and effective articles on such environmentally destructive practices as strip mining, channelization, unethical use of aircraft to take trophy game, political interference in wildlife affairs, the indiscriminate use of pesticides and the damming of wild and scenic rivers and streams.

In 1973, he was signally honored when the Michigan Senate and House of Representatives adopted a concurrent resolution, the legislature's highest tribute, recognizing him for his distinguished contribution to the conservation of natural resources.

A FOREWORD
TO GRIZZLY!

Was Napier Shelton to blame in any way for the savage attack the grizzly bear made on him? What could he have done that caused its rage and made it come after him so fiercely?

The answer is unknown.

There are three times when a grizzly is very dangerous. One is when a person, not knowing the bear is there, gets too close. The grizzly may decide the person is looking for a fight, or believes itself to be cornered. Another is when a she bear has cubs with her. She will protect them angrily from any danger, real or imagined. The third is when a man comes close to a bear that is guarding its food. It does not matter whether the food is prey the grizzly has killed or a dead animal it has found and started to eat. It will not give up its food without a fight. The human may not know there is a bear in the area, but the grizzly will have smelled or heard the person coming, and be waiting to attack. Now and then this bear even kills a human for food.

None of these three things happened in Shelton's case. He saw no cubs, the bear came for him out of the woods where it had plenty of room, and there was no sign it had been feeding nearby. The attack was not caused by a human. It simply happened because the grizzly found a man in its home area and decided to kill him.

The grizzly is hot-tempered, unpredictable, and very dangerous. It has killed many people since white man first invaded its homeland in the West almost two hundred years ago. The bear has attacked and mauled more than it has killed.

An old Montana game warden, who had dealt with troublemaking grizzlies all his life, once told me that a man is never safe for a minute in places where the grizzly is found. Napier Shelton's story proves that the old warden was right.

BEN EAST

Napier Shelton wanted to meet a grizzly bear. He wanted to meet it face-to-face, in the wild. Growing up in Washington D.C. did not provide him with the opportunity to see a live bear except at the zoo or in a circus. But Shelton had read a book on wild grizzlies. Since then, he had longed to get to know such a bear firsthand. When he was twenty-nine years old, he got his chance. He never dreamed it might try to kill him!

Shelton was a college student in North Carolina and was studying botany, the science of plant life. He and a friend, Jack Van Wyk, wanted to get away from their books for a while, so they decided to spend the summer in Alaska. For Shelton, such a summer would be a dream come true. Shelton had wanted to see that part of the country for a long time. While there, he would be studying the plants of the far north as a school project. However, it was the wild animals that he wanted to see most. There would be plenty of grizzly bears up there. Jack had no part in the school project but was going on the trip just to see the country. Being from South Africa, a trip such as this would take him about as far away from home as he would ever get. Jack planned to stay with Shelton for only two weeks. Then he would fly back to school to work on his own studies.

The two men spent the springtime fixing up Shelton's small camping van. The rear seat was ripped out, and in its place a table was built that could also serve as a bed. They stocked the van with canned food, planning to camp along the way. Late in May the two men set out on the 4,900 mile drive. They were on no schedule and would simply pull off the road when night came to eat and sleep.

The men reached Mt. McKinley National Park early in June. The first night they were there Shelton went for a walk by himself along the Toklat River. Here he saw his first grizzly bear track. Placing his boot beside the track he found the paw marks were almost as long as his own footprint, and a lot wider. The mark of four-inch claws was plain and clear in the wet sand. Shelton lifted his head and looked around. There was a light rain falling, and the clouds were low. Mist veiled the entire valley. It gave a gloomy look to the trees and the dark mountains. All of a sudden, Shelton felt small and alone. The wish to meet a grizzly bear face-to-face, the wish that had been in his heart for so many years, seemed to vanish. He was sure the maker of the track could not be far away. In the fading light, with the mist closing in, each shadow looked like a grizzly. He turned around quickly and started walking back to the van. He walked faster than usual. This was neither the time nor the place to meet such a bear.

Shelton had regained his courage by the time he got to the van. He told Jack about the track as they drove to the park campground at Igloo Creek. Seeing the track had not stopped Shelton from wanting to meet a grizzly bear face-to-face. However, it gave him second thoughts. Since the men were in a national park, it was not legal for them to have guns. Shelton would not have brought one anyway. He did not believe that wild animals would bother humans unless they were given a good reason. Shelton did not intend to give the bears he met a reason to bother him, but would meet them as friends. He was sure they would do the same. In the books he had read, it said that the grizzly only attacks man when provoked.

Jack did not share Shelton's view of wild animals. He had seen things at home that had taught him a different lesson. Wild creatures of many kinds can be dangerous, at times for no good reason. Once a cobra snake spit venom in his eyes which blinded him for awhile. Another time, a deadly mamba snake reared up to Jack's face. He shot the head off just as it was ready to strike. His father killed a leopard with an ax as it came at him. And once, while on a hunt, Jack met some bushmen in a tree. A lion had just killed one of their group and fed on the body. Such things had made Jack cautious with animals so he always carried a hatchet. It was not much of a weapon, and would have been worthless against a grizzly. Still, he felt safer with it.

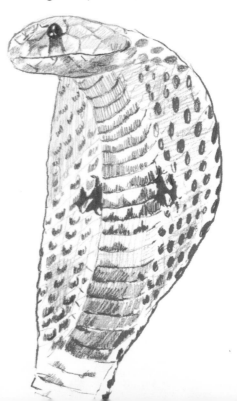

11

At the Igloo Creek campground the men pitched their tent and settled down to enjoy the country. The two weeks together went by all too quickly. After Jack left for school Shelton was alone in the wild, but it did not bother him. He began to see a lot of grizzlies; so many, in fact, they became a common part of the landscape. There were few near the campground, but at the head of Igloo Creek six or more were sometimes seen on the same day. He could watch them from his van while traveling the gravel road that ran through the park. Some were dark brown, the color of chocolate. Others were a light blond color. The contrast was so great it was often startling.

During the first weeks Shelton was alone, the grizzlies he saw were all at a distance. They were beautiful and he enjoyed watching them. He watched the mothers and their cubs with special interest. The cubs were cute and full of mischief. The mothers nursed them contentedly. If they sensed danger, they quickly became vicious. Shelton was learning an important lesson. The grizzly knows he is king of his territory and shows it. He prowls with a proud, powerful look and walks with a slow, bow-legged strut. He retreats only from man, but does not like to. As the summer wore on, Shelton heard more and more stories of those who had met grizzlies face-to-face. He began to question his belief that bears were peaceful unless provoked.

13

Joe Hankins, one of the campers at Igloo Creek, got a good scare from a grizzly one day. After coming back to camp he told Shelton all about it. Joe worked for a big logging outfit on the West Coast. Each summer for nine years he quit his job and came north for a long rest. He liked to hike and take pictures. Joe had seen many bears in those nine years, and the two men had often talked about them. The day Joe got too close to one, it came at him with no warning. He was lucky since it only chased him a short distance and quit. Shelton had also heard a story about a grizzly that, for no reason, took a swing at a man standing on his back porch. And there were many stories of the unlucky hunters,

guides and prospectors who never lived to tell their stories.

Shelton still did not believe grizzlies would attack unless provoked. He was not afraid of them and wanted to meet one face-to-face. The only precaution he took was to carry a beer can half-full of small stones. When the can was rattled it made a lot of noise. He had been told a loud noise would scare a bear away if one got too close. The can was with him at all times!

As the blueberries ripened in July, there were more and more grizzly sightings. The bears came down from the high country to be near the berries. Shelton often saw them on the slopes where he was working. The willow and birch grew so thick there that the bear trails became tunnels. To get through, a man had to follow the paths made by the bears. It gave Shelton a strange feeling, as if he were on "private" property.

One day he walked out of such a tunnel to see a big, blond bear just a few yards down the mountain from him! He stopped and stared at the big brute. It was so busy eating berries it did not see him. Since the wind was blowing uphill, it could not smell him. He was lucky! There could have been trouble, right then-and-there.

Shelton watched the bear long enough to learn that a grizzly, at close range, gives a real sense of power and danger. For the first time, he felt the risk involved in meeting one of these bears. He backed carefully out of the bear's sight and retreated about fifty yards. Then he rattled his beer can as loudly as possible. It worked! The bear stopped picking berries, looked up and sniffed the air. Then, without looking back, it ran off quickly. The whole thing took just a few minutes. It took much longer for Shelton's heart to beat normally again!

Back at camp that night, he was warned that another mother bear with two cubs had been sighted on Igloo Mountain. Shelton had seen

19

enough that day. He knew that if he and the bear should meet, he would give her plenty of room to run.

The rest of the month passed smoothly, with Shelton doing his plant studies daily. During the first few days of August it rained, so he stayed in his tent. The fourth day dawned sunny and warm. After so much rain, Shelton was eager to get back to his studies. He parked the van on the road above the campground and walked across Igloo Creek on a fallen log. He wanted to get tree borings from the creek to the timber line. These would tell him the age of each tree. It was three hundred yards from the creek to timber line, so he had a lot of work to do. The day was bright and still, with only a light breeze in the treetops. Shelton liked working in the peaceful forest. By midday he had worked his way to the edge of the timber. While poking through a very dense thicket of brush, he found first a four-inch tree, and then an eight-inch one. He took borings from each of them. Then he saw a spruce at least a foot wide. It was the thickest tree in sight, but only about twenty feet tall. Its branches were twisted and scraggly, and there were many willows around it. Leaving his pack on the ground, he pushed through the brush to the tree. There he sat down and went to work with his boring tool.

Suddenly, the stillness was shattered by a loud and vicious "WARF!" It was a sound of surprise and rage, a half bark and half snarl. It came from a few steps below him, down the slope where his pack was. Shelton knew what it was without looking. Moving quickly, he reached for the nearest branch of the scraggly spruce, and climbed the tree as if he were a squirrel. If he could only get out of the bear's reach before it grabbed for him, he would be safe! He had read and been told that grizzlies do not climb trees once they are adults.

He was eight or ten feet up the tree before looking down. What he saw made him gasp. A large, snarling grizzly bear was scrambling awkwardly up after him—and it was coming fast! The branches grew like the rungs of a ladder which seemed to be helping the bear. Shelton reached for another branch above his head. As he pulled himself up, he could feel the bear grab the calf of his leg. Its teeth ripped loose a big flap of skin and muscle, but Shelton felt no pain. Again, he tried to pull himself out of the bear's reach. This time the bear's teeth caught him by the heel of his boot. The weight of the bear on his foot was loosening his hold and pulling him down. Branches broke in his hands and under his free foot. It felt as if he were falling into a bottomless pit.

"This is it!" he thought.

Suddenly, the pull on his foot was gone. He heard a crash and a thud, and looking down the grizzly could be seen tumbling through the branches to the ground. Shelton was frantic. He started climbing higher, but almost at once he felt the whole tree shake. He knew the bear was coming up after him once more. He had only a few more branches left above his head, and the bear was still climbing. He could see it just below his feet. It was the most terrifying thing Shelton had ever seen. The coarse blond hair on its head and shoulders was standing straight up. Its yellow teeth were bared in a savage snarl. Its small eyes were blazing. As it climbed, it continued to growl. It was straining every muscle to reach him.

For a moment, Shelton was angry. This bear had no fear of him as a human. It was trying to kill him as it would kill any animal it had treed or cornered. It had no business acting this way, Shelton thought. The books all said bears do not attack man unless provoked. He certainly had done nothing to provoke this one.

He smashed his boot down on its head. It did no more good than kicking a brick wall. Shelton's anger changed to disbelief. His mind would not accept the fact that he was being attacked by a grizzly bear.

Teeth slashed into him again, this time high in his right thigh. Again, he felt no pain. The bear bit down hard but then it lost its grip in the branches. It let go of his leg and went tumbling to the ground for the second time. Shelton watched it, knowing he was as high as he could climb in the scraggly spruce. If it came for him again, he could get no higher. For a few long minutes it walked slowly around the tree, snorting and growling. But it did not try to climb after him a third time. At last, still snarling, it moved off slowly into the willows. As it left, it gave Shelton a look that said: "I'm not through with you yet!"

Up to this point, there had not been much time for Shelton to think. The whole attack had been so sudden and vicious, he had been helpless. There had been no warning—no breaking of brush, no sound of movement. Shelton had acted on instinct. He was sure the bear would pull him out of the tree and kill him. However, he lost his fear after it grabbed him the first time.

As he began to relax, his breathing returned to normal, and pain could be felt in his legs. He was shaking very hard, and was quickly getting weaker. Shelton was still in the top of the scrawny spruce, and was getting very tired of holding onto the branches. The grizzly was still in the brush nearby, waiting for him, he was sure. As he looked down at his legs, he could see a row of tooth holes in his right thigh and a torn chunk of flesh hanging from his left calf. His trousers were hanging in bloody rags. Weak as he was, Shelton did not dare climb down from the tree. His strength was failing fast. He could not stay in the tree much longer, no matter what danger awaited him on the ground.

At the foot of the slope he could see his van parked on the road. Three hundred yards of forest separated him from the safety of the van. As he looked at it longingly, a car drove past. He yelled loudly, but the distance was too great. The driver could not hear him.

Shelton was tired. He waited about twenty minutes. Then he could not stay in the tree any longer. Carefully, step by step, he climbed down. Terror gripped him every inch of the way. Any second he feared the grizzly would come charging at him. He put one foot on the ground, looked around at the brush around him, and lost his nerve. The grizzly was still there, he just knew it. Back he climbed, up and up, as high as he could go in the scraggly spruce. Shelton tried to peer into the thicket for some sign of the bear. He yelled and rattled his can of stones. There was no response. He did not know where in the thick brush it was, or if it were still there. A second car passed on the road while he stared into the thicket, and again he shouted for help. It drove on, not knowing he was there.

He was growing very weak. He knew he could not stay in the tree any longer, whether the bear was waiting for him on the ground or not. It would be better to get down while he could still climb. He did not want to risk getting hurt more by falling. He climbed down slowly --- watching, listening, hardly breathing. Nothing happened. Once on the ground, he grabbed his hat and headed for the road as fast as his wounds would let him. He yelled and made as much noise as he could as he broke through the

brush from the tree to the road. Each second he expected to see the big shaggy brute come roaring at him.

But it didn't.

To Shelton, it seemed like it took a lifetime to get back to Igloo Creek. He slid down the bank, splashed across the creek, and climbed to the road. There still were two hundred yards between him and the van. He tried to run, but could not. The thought of the grizzly closing in haunted him each

painful step. Reaching the van, he crawled quickly inside and slammed the door.

"Thank God!" he said aloud. It was over, and he was safe.

As Shelton sat in the van trying to think, he saw a green jeep coming up the road. It was Adolph Murie, a Park Service biologist who had been studying grizzly bears for years.

"One of your friends bit me!" Shelton shouted out the window at Murie.

The man spun his jeep around and pulled up beside the van. Shelton told him about the attack and showed him his wounds. Murie could not take care of the wounds out there on the road. The two men talked while Shelton calmed himself. Then Murie asked him if he could still drive. Weak as he was, Shelton believed he could. He started the van, and set out slowly for the campgound while Murie followed in his jeep. His cabin was just across the road from where Shelton's tent was pitched. As soon as they got there, Murie and his wife gave Shelton first aid. Then they drove him thirty miles to the park hotel. There, a nurse bandaged his wounds and gave him a tetanus shot. She looked through the guest list to see if a doctor was staying at the hotel, but there was none. So she phoned for a bush plane to take him to a hospital in Fairbanks. Shelton had to borrow a pair of pants for the flight. His own were too torn and bloody to wear.

At the hospital, Dr. Haggland took care of Shelton's wounds. Dr. Haggland was a hunter, and had seen many bears himself. As a surgeon he had also seen many injuries from bears. He talked about some of them while he sewed up Shelton's wounds.

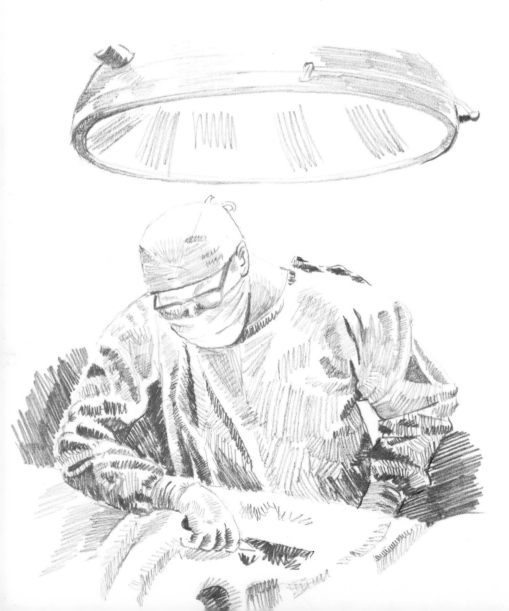

When he was done, he summed up Shelton's thoughts in three words: "You were lucky!"

The calf of Shelton's left leg was badly torn. The bear's teeth had left deep puncture wounds in his right thigh. His heel, where the bear had bit through his boot, was not badly hurt. There was no bone damage anywhere. Shelton also had a few other cuts on his body, but nothing serious. The bear had not used its claws. Perhaps it had needed them to hang onto the tree. If it had, Shelton might not have been so lucky!

Shelton stayed in the hospital for five days. Then he went back to the park hotel. After a few more days of rest, he, the Muries, and two other friends went to the scene of the attack. Shelton wanted to find some of the tools he had left behind. There was a lump in his throat each step of the way. In his mind, there was a bear behind each bush. But not one was sighted. The Muries told him that park rangers had searched the thicket the day after the attack. They had seen no bear either.

Shelton easily found the spruce that had saved his life. It had bear hair clinging to its branches four-teen feet above the ground. Big limbs had broken

off where the grizzly had fought its way up the tree and fallen twice to the ground. It was proof of what Shelton had known all along. The grizzly climbed the tree and did not just stand on its hind feet and reach up at him with its front paws.

Shelton stayed on with the Muries for two more weeks while regaining his strength. Then he set out for home in his van. He had met his grizzly bear and he would never forget it!

Shelton will never know for sure what caused the vicious attack. The bear was blond, the same color as the mother with cubs that had been seen on Igloo Mountain right before the attack. However, there were many bears of that color in the park. There is no easy way of telling one bear from another. Shelton had seen no cubs, and could not tell the sex of the grizzly that mauled him. Some of the park rangers think the bear just happened to walk out of the brush where Shelton had left his pack. Startled by the smell of it, the bear flew into instant rage. Others think it might have heard the squeaking of his boring tool. Thinking the sound came from some small animal in trouble, it went looking for food. All they can do is guess. The reason for the attack is still a mystery.

What happened to the bear is a mystery, too. As far as Shelton knows, no one ever saw it again.

At home, Shelton reread some of his books. He found this quote about grizzlies:

"This bear never climbs. The
hunter who succeeds in getting
up a tree is as safe from a
grizzly as from a bull."

Shelton stared at the quote for a long time, and shook his head in disbelief. "Anyone who believes that should have been with me that day on Igloo Creek!"

Shelton may have thought he was through with bears in the wild. But he liked the outdoors, and he was bound to meet one again some day.

After college, Shelton found a teaching job in Michigan. One summer, he and his wife went on a canoe trip in Canada. It had been four years since the grizzly attack. Their first night out, they camped at a site where other campers had been not too long before. Someone had buried garbage, and a black bear had found it. It came into camp each night and dug up a feast. The Shelton's did not know the garbage was there, and pitched their tent just a few feet away. They hung their food pack between two trees and crawled into their sleeping bags.

Shortly after dark, the bear came into camp. It smelled the food in the packs and went after them first. But, try as it might, the bear could not pull the packs down. It was so close to the tent, Shelton could hear its heavy breathing. He remembered his beer can full of stones, so tried to make enough noise to scare it away. He yelled and banged on anything he could find in the tent. It worked. The bear moved away from the packs. But then it started digging up the garbage. It walked slowly around the tent, grunting and grumbling. In spite of all Shelton did, the bear stayed for the rest of the night.

Later, Shelton said, "I did not sleep a wink until it left at dawn. I don't think I have ever had a worse night. I will never trust any bear again as long as I live!"

Stay on the edge of your seat.

Read:

FROZEN TERROR

DANGER IN THE AIR

MISTAKEN JOURNEY

TRAPPED IN DEVIL'S HOLE

DESPERATE SEARCH

FORTY DAYS LOST

FOUND ALIVE

GRIZZLY!

SURVIVAL TRUE STORIES